Places I  Love to Go

By Wade Hudson • Illustrated by Laura Freeman

MARIMBA BOOKS
An imprint of Kensington Publishing Corp. and Hudson Publishing Group LLC
850 Third Avenue, New York, NY 10022

Text copyright © 2008 by Wade Hudson. Illustrations copyright © 2008 by Laura Freeman.

All Kensington titles, imprints, and distributed lines are available at special quantity discounts for bulk purchases for sales promotions,
premiums, fund-raising, and educational or institutional use.

Special book excerpts or customized printings can also be created to fit specific needs.
For details, write or phone the office of the Kensington special sales manager:
Kensington Publishing Corp., 850 Third Avenue, New York, NY 10022, attn: Special Sales Department, 1-800-221-2647.

MARIMBA BOOKS and the Marimba Books logo are trademarks of Kensington Publishing Corp. and Hudson Publishing Group LLC.

ISBN-13: 978-1-60349-008-5   ISBN-10: 1-60349-008-6
First Marimba Books printing: September 2008

10 9 8 7 6 5 4 3 2 1

Printed in the United States of America

There are many places I love to go.
They're fun. That's why I love them so.

I love running in the park
and swinging on the swing.

I love going to school

Where I learn new things.

There's excitement at the park.

I zoom down the slide!

Visiting Grandpa's house is great.

There are wonderful places to hide.

I love the ice cream truck.

The Popsicles are cool.

I love to splash about

in the neighborhood pool.

Scary movies make my heart pound.

Popcorn tastes good while
I'm watching the circus clown.

The zoo has animals that I love to feed.

The library is a special place
where I go to read.

At the rink I do tricks
on *my* brand new skates.

Ummmm! Mrs. Diaz's bakery sells my favorite cake.

I play next door with my best friend Ray.